Based on the screenplay by Mike Werb
Story by Michael Fallon
and Mark Verheiden

Turner Publishing, Inc.
ATLANTA

Published by Turner Publishing, Inc.
A Subsidiary of Turner Broadcasting System, Inc.
1050 Techwood Drive, N.W.
Atlanta, Georgia 30318

Library of Congress Cataloging-in-Publication Data
Fallon, Michael, 1957–
   The Mask: based on the screenplay by Mike Werb/story by Michael Fallon and Mark Verheiden.
         p.   cm.
Summary: Stanley, a young bank clerk, finds an ancient mask that gives him amazing powers.
ISBN 1-57036-162-2
   [1. Supernatural–Fiction.]   I. Verheiden, Mark.   II. Werb, Mike.   III. Title.
PZ7.F196Mas   1995
[Fic]–dc20   94-42984
                                                                                   CIP
                                                                                   AC

Distributed in the U.S. by: Distributed in the UK by:
Andrews and McMeel   Pegasus Sales and Distribution Ltd.
A Universal Press Syndicate Company   Unit 5B, Causeway Park
4900 Main Street   Wilderspool Causeway
Kansas City, Missouri 64112   Warrington, Cheshire WA4 6QE

Editor–Zodie Spain
Design–Robert Zides and Michael J. Walsh
Picture Editor–Marty Moore
Production–Christine Holmes

First Edition 10 9 8 7 6 5 4 3 2 1

Printed in the U.S.A.

Hold the phone, killer at 3:00!

That's an interesting tie, Mr. Ipkiss.

Everyone takes advantage of Stanley Ipkiss, a friendly young accounts clerk at the Edge City Savings and Loan. One rainy afternoon at the bank, Stanley and his best friend, Charlie Schumacher, are excited by the sudden appearance of Tina Carlyle, the singing sensation of the trendy new Coco Bongo nightclub. Though she appears to be interested in discussing a new account with Stanley, she is secretly videotaping the bank vault for her mobster boyfriend, Dorian Tyrel.

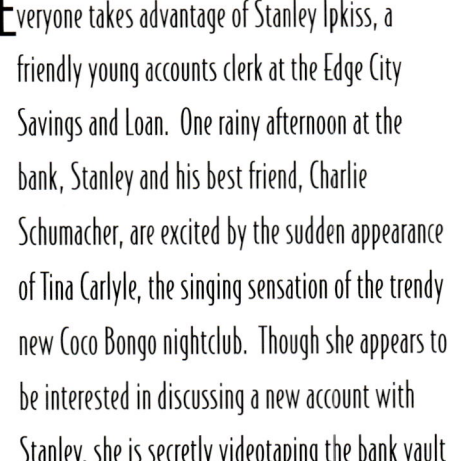

That's it, sweetheart—just a little bit to the right.

I was just looking for...

L ater that night, after embarrassing himself in front of Tina at the Coco Bongo, Stanley is driving home across a bridge when his miserable car (a loaner from a couple of shifty mechanics) breaks down. Alarmed by what appears to be a body floating in the river, Stanley leaps to the rescue, but finds only some debris and a strange, ancient mask. The police arrive and question Stanley.

Hey you! What are you doing down there?

my mask.

The cops drop Stanley off at home where he finds Milo, his faithful dog, waiting for him. Stressed out, Stanley tries to unwind by watching cartoons and playing Frisbee with Milo, but has to stop when his landlady, Mrs. Peenman, complains about the noise. Stanley decides to turn in, but cannot resist first trying on the mysterious mask.

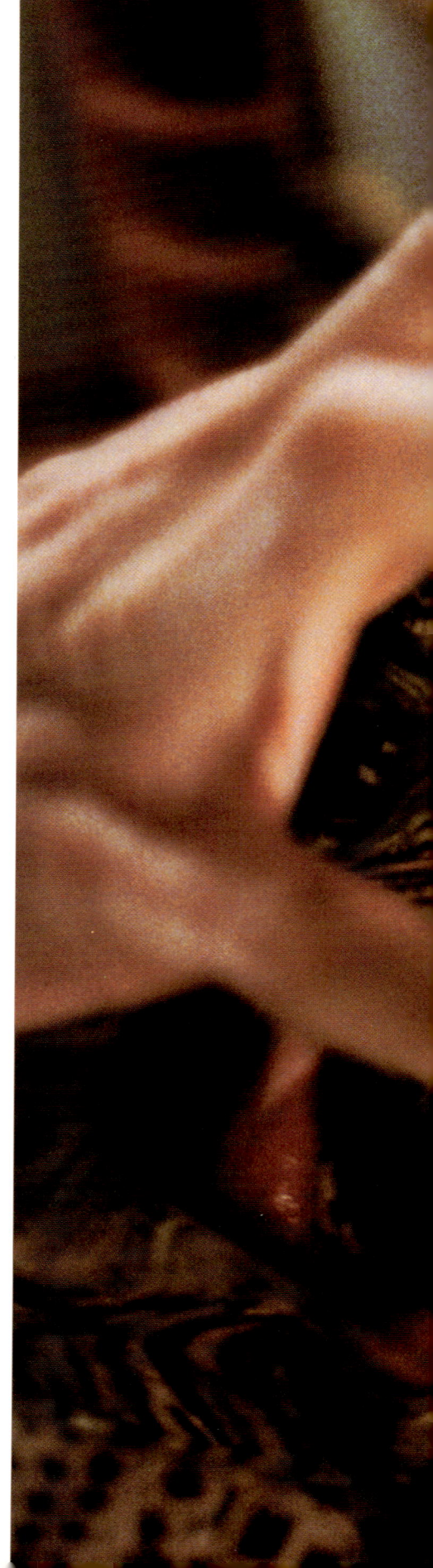

As the mask's fantastic magical powers whirl Stanley around the apartment like a crazed tornado, Milo cowers in fear. Coming to an abrupt stop, Stanley grooves on his cool, new hipster identity, The Mask, and decides to step out for an extra special night on the town.

smokin'!

P-A-R-T-whY?. Because I gotta!

In the hall outside Mrs. Peenman's door, The Mask tries be quiet, but a ringing alarm clock suddenly leaps from his jacket pocket and bounces up and down the hallway, giggling madly. Pulling a large sledgehammer from his pocket, The Mask makes a frenzied attempt to smash the clock. An indignant Mrs. Peenman throws open her door, catches sight of The Mask, and both of them scream wildly at the sight of one another.

ZZZZZZZZ snooze! ZZZZ

Look ma,
I'm

To Mrs. Peenman's horror, The Mask careens around the hallway and escapes by exiting through the window at the far end. He plummets to the street below and is flattened like a pancake, but simply peels himself off the pavement.

roadkill

municate.

The Mask finds himself in the middle of the street and is confronted by an angry motorist who wants him to move out of the way. In response, The Mask squeezes a little horn and unleashes a devastatingly loud sonic blast.

Sorry, wrong pocket.

Here's a giraffe for you...

...a French poodle,

Next, The Mask runs into a bunch of street punks on the prowl for a victim. The Mask first distracts the hoodlums with a charming display of balloon art. He then produces an all too real tommy gun, and runs them off with a spray of bullets.

and my favorite... a

tommy gun!

This is incredible! With these powers I could fight crime, protect the innocent, work for world peace...

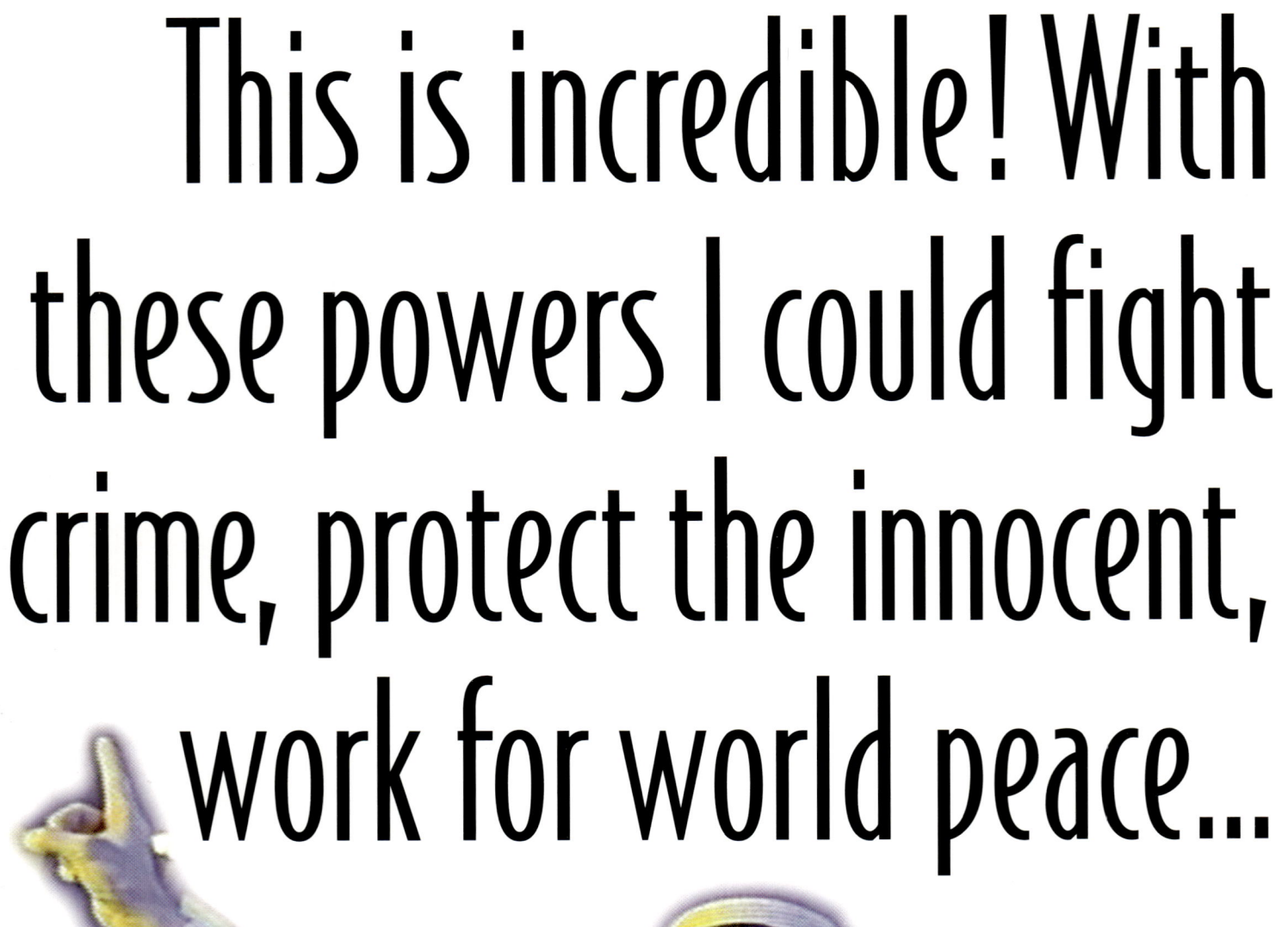

Exhilarated by his incredible new-found abilities, The Mask decides on his next course of action. He heads for the auto shop to avenge himself on the mechanics who ripped him off earlier that day.

but(t) first. . .

This is my personal number.

The next morning, Stanley is questioned by Lt. Kellaway, who is investigating Mrs. Peenman's report of a strange intruder. Kellaway is suspicious of Stanley but leaves him alone—for now. Across town, Dorian Tyrel is confronted by gang boss Niko, who doesn't appreciate Dorian's business dealings at the Coco Bongo and threatens to kill him if he doesn't leave town soon. Later at the bank, Stanley is visited by Peggy Brandt, a reporter looking into the previous night's bizarre events at the auto shop.

If you mess with Niko, you end up taking a dirt nap.

Hold on sugar, Daddy's got a sweet tooth tonight!

Stanley dreams about Tina, but wakes up convinced that someone like her could never be interested in a zero like himself. On an impulse, he grabs the mask and puts it on. Now changed into his slick, debonair alter ego, he is primed to hit the Coco Bongo and win Tina over.

She would never—no way!

Can't make the scene if you don't have the

Deciding to make an unauthorized withdrawal on the way, The Mask runs into Dorian's gang at the bank, and wrecks their heist-in-progress. He then heads straight to the Coco Bongo for the main event.

How do! Meet my friends, Franklin, Grant, and Jackson.

green.

Gee, baby, ain't I good to you.

That's my girl, the flower of the Coco Bongo.

At the club, Tina is onstage, singing her heart out. Seated at his ringside table, The Mask cannot take his eyes off of her.

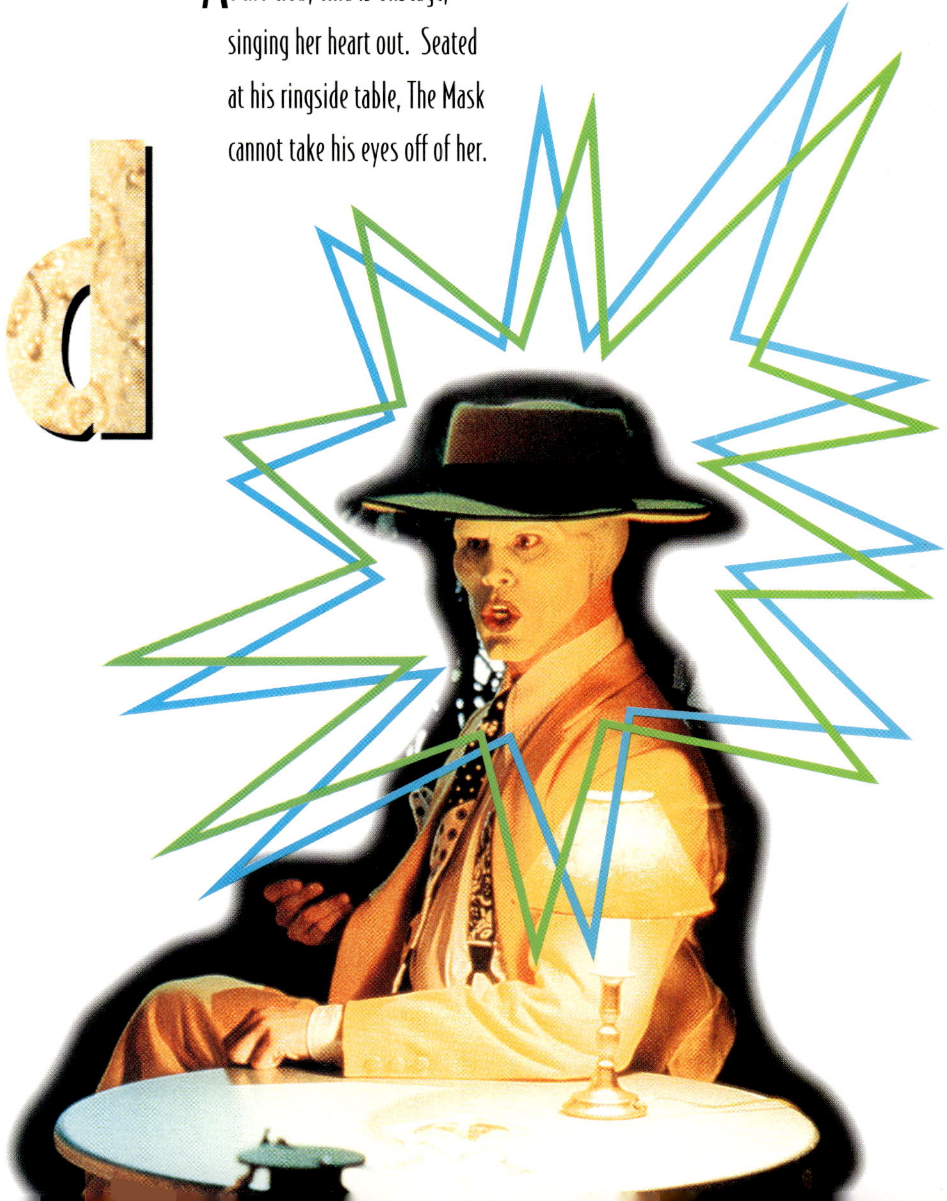

Smokin'!

Let's rock this joint!

Driven completely wild by Tina's performance, The Mask jumps onto the dance floor and performs a wacky jitterbug with her, jiving at warp speed.

ice

When Dorian finds out that The Mask is responsible for the failure of his gang's heist, he unsuccessfully attempts to shoot him on the dance floor. Just then, Lt. Kellaway bursts in with the police to arrest Dorian for the bank job, and The Mask escapes. As the cops haul Dorian away, Kellaway finds a piece of fabric from The Mask's tie and recognizes it as the same material from which Stanley's outrageous pajamas are made.

him!

Our love is like

I am a little

You and the Mask are one and the same beautiful person.

a red, red rose, and thorny.

At the bank the next day, Tina tells Stanley about her great attraction to The Mask. He agrees to set up a meeting between them at Landfill Park that evening, then consults a prominent psychiatrist because he is not sure how to approach Tina. Armed with the doctor's advice to go to his rendezvous as both The Mask and himself, Stanley meets Tina at the park. Once The Mask makes his appearance and begins to romance her, Tina is flattered but also frightened by his extreme attentions.

freeze

Let's get him!

K ellaway has followed Stanley to the park and is now certain that he is The Mask and is responsible for all the recent crimes. Deciding to make his move, he and his partner rush from their hiding place. While the Lieutenant attempts to detain and question The Mask, Tina escapes. The Mask makes a run for the park gates, closing and securing them behind him in the hope that he will be safe from the police.

I have a permit for that.

hit it!

Turning around, The Mask sees what looks like the entire police force waiting for him. Cornered, with nowhere to turn, he creates a big, splashy musical number and compels all the cops to participate.

When I put on that mask, I can do or be anything.

The Mask slips down an alleyway. Though Kellaway is hot on his trail, he manages to elude the Lieutenant long enough to pull off the mask and hop into Peggy Brandt's car. Peggy takes him to the newspaper offices where Dorian and his men show up. Dorian pays Peggy off for betraying Stanley and takes possession of the mask. When he puts it on, the mobster becomes more evil than ever.

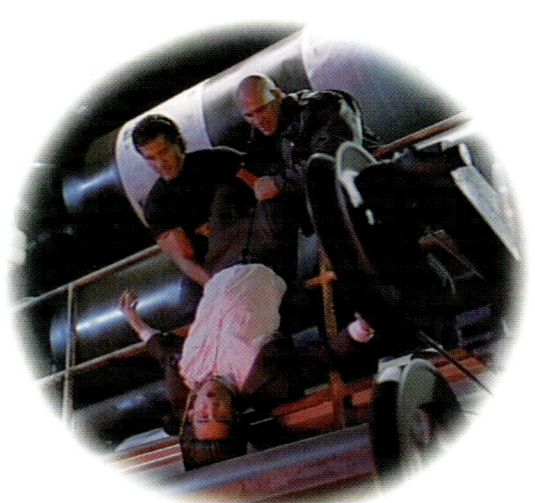

What a *rush*.

What's Dorian gonna do, the lambada?

It was you I wanted all along – the guy inside the mask.

Dorian and his men force Stanley to give them the money from the bank robbery and then dump him outside police headquarters. Stanley is immediately arrested by Kellaway. Milo, having followed from the apartment, sits outside of Stanley's cell window. The next morning, Tina visits Stanley in jail and confides that her interest is in him rather than The Mask, and that she is very worried that Dorian is planning something big at the Coco Bongo that night. After she leaves, Milo helps free Stanley, who then forces Kellaway at gunpoint to lead him out of police headquarters.

payback

Dorian, as The Mask, forces Tina to accompany him—with a box of dynamite—to the Coco Bongo. Leaving Kellaway and Milo locked in the car outside the club, Stanley sneaks in to stop Dorian/Mask and rescue Tina. Milo manages to get out of the car and runs after Stanley. Inside, Dorian/Mask kills Niko in a showdown and breaks open a giant piggy bank filled with money.

Please, just one last kiss. Nobody ever kissed me like Dorian Tyrel.

M

Dorian/Mask ties Tina to a tree by the ornamental pool and sets a timer attached to the dynamite. Tina convinces him to take off the mask by begging for one last kiss, and when he does, she kicks it out of his hand. As Stanley fights with Dorian, the mask flies through the club and everyone scrambles after it. Just as one of the thugs is about to grab the mask, Milo sails through the air and catches it like a Frisbee.

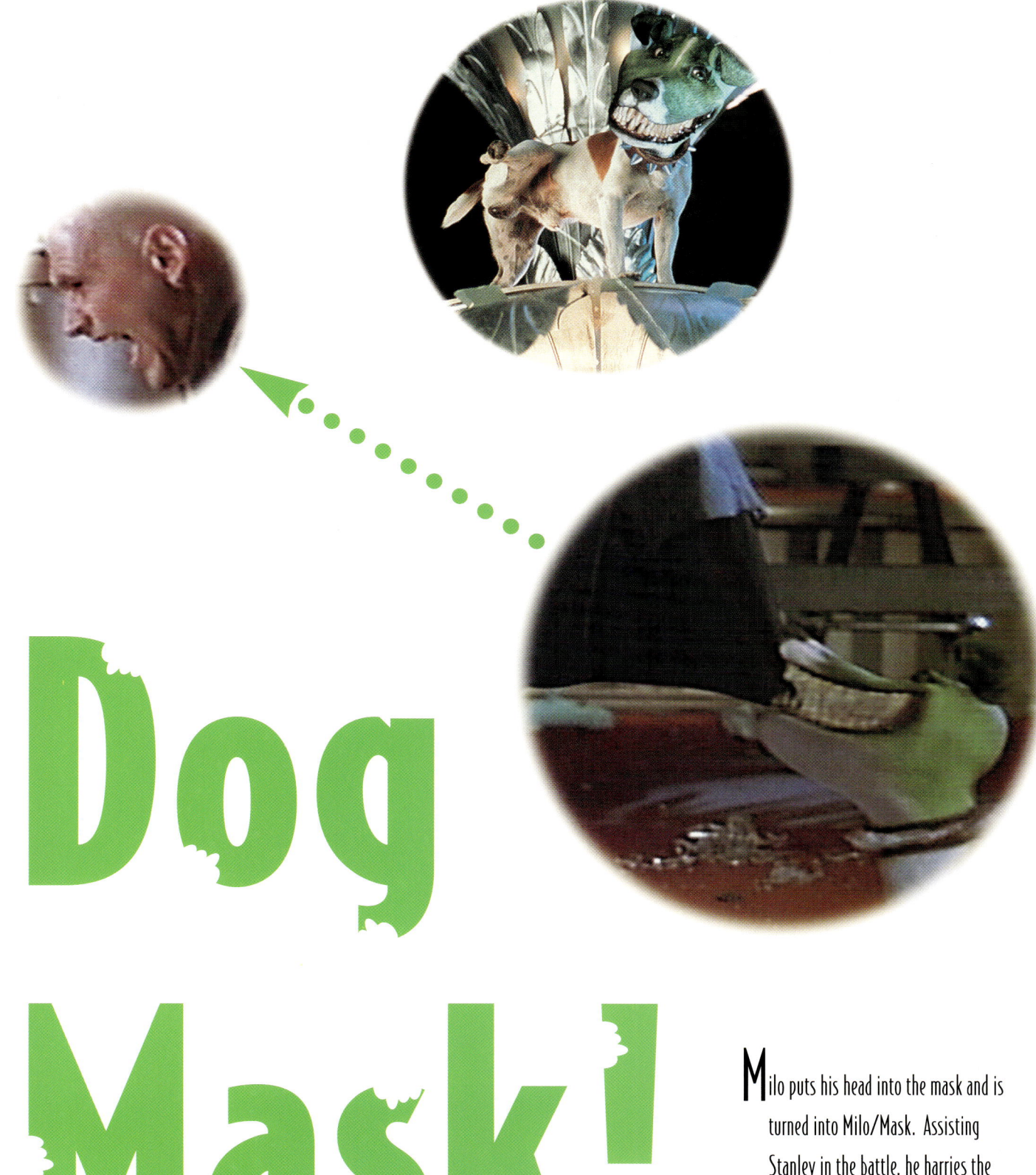

Dog Mask!

Milo puts his head into the mask and is turned into Milo/Mask. Assisting Stanley in the battle, he harries the thugs as only a Masked dog can.

Stanley clobbers Dorian, grabs Milo, and pulls the mask off of the dog. Putting it on himself, he disappears momentarily behind the bar, which the thugs promptly spray with bullets. Convinced he is dead, they are surprised when The Mask suddenly emerges as a 40's tough guy.

Did you miss me?

I guess not!

Facing down the terrified gangsters, The Mask whips out a huge array of weapons, including rocket launchers. This is too much for the thugs, and they run out of the Coco Bongo.

Do you

feel **lucky**, punks?

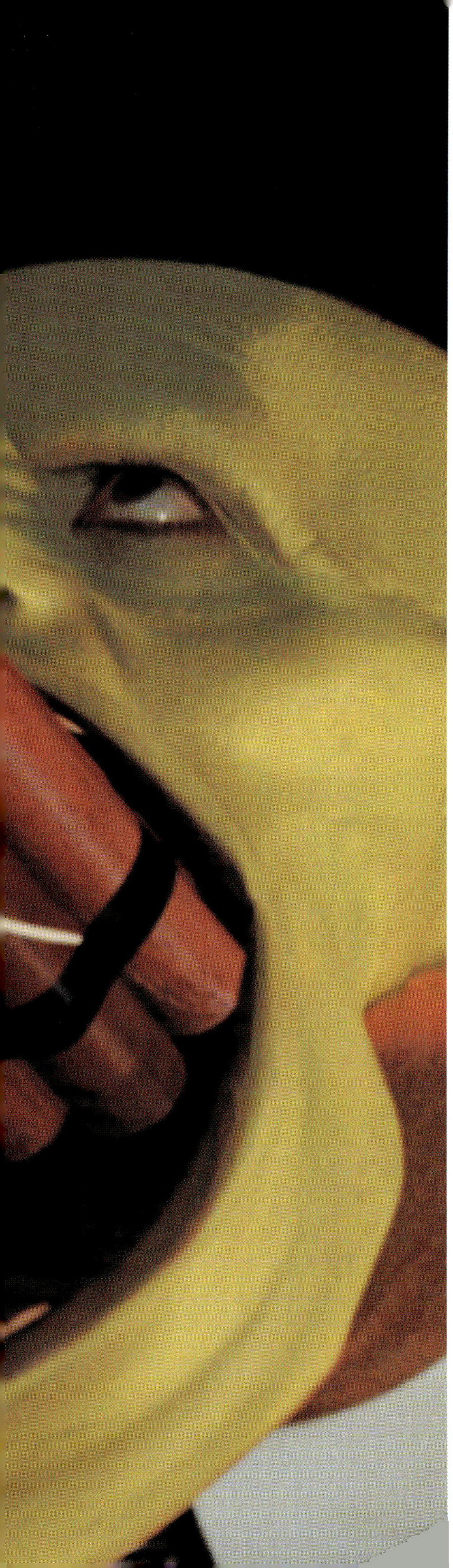

That'sa spicy meatball!

T ina and the entire club are still in danger from the ticking bomb. The Mask zooms over and swallows the entire package, which explodes harmlessly inside his stomach.

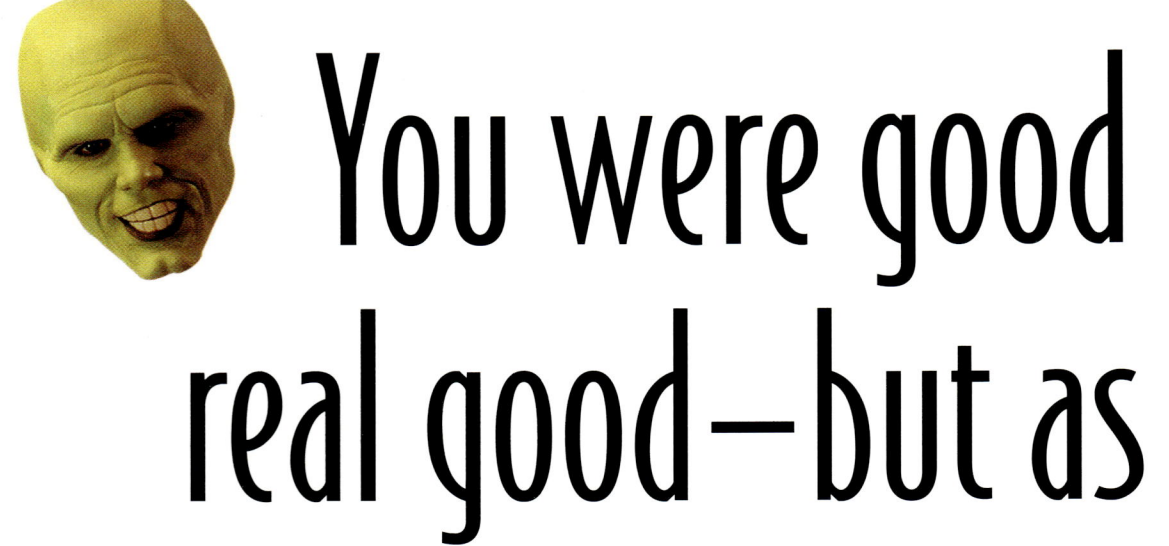

You were good kid, real good—but as long as I'm around, you'll always be second best.

Dorian is not about to accept defeat, and he rushes toward The Mask with a knife, intending to fight to the end. The Mask quickly produces an artist's palette and paints a giant toilet handle on the tree. He pulls the handle down, and the ensuing giant whirlpool flushes Dorian down the drain, eliminating him for good. The crisis over, the mayor of Edge City insists that all charges against Stanley be dropped completely and that Dorian be charged with the crimes, thereby closing Kellaway's investigation.

Are you sure you know what you're doing, Stanley?

A new day dawns over Edge City as Stanley drives with Tina, Milo, and his best friend Charlie to the bridge to dispose of the mask. When Stanley hesitates, Tina throws the mask off the bridge herself and they kiss. Sneaking out of the car down to the river, Charlie jumps in to retrieve the mask. Much to his dismay, Milo effortlessly paddles past him, the mask firmly clenched between his teeth.

sm♥kin!

acknowledgments

Turner Publishing would like to thank the many people at New Line
whose invaluable assistance and input made this project possible.

We especially would like to extend our appreciation
to David Imhoff and Judith Verno for their support and enthusiasm.
In Los Angeles, we would like to thank Helene Steel,
and particularly Tod Abrams and his staff,
including Fran Hawkins, Chris Pula, and Travis Topa, who
fulfilled our requests for visual materials with efficiency and professionalism.

picture credits